CHICAGOLAND
DETECTIVE AGENCY

N°6

A Midterm Night's Scheme

TRINA ROBBINS
ILLUSTRATED BY TYLER PAGE

GRAPHIC UNIVERSE™ • MINNEAPOLIS

STORY BY **TRINA ROBBINS**

PENCILS AND INKS BY **TYLER PAGE**

LETTERING BY **ZACK GIALLONGO**

COVER COLORING BY **HI-FI DESIGN**

Graphic Universe™
A division of Lerner Publishing Group, Inc.
241 First Avenue North
Minneapolis, MN 55401 USA

For reading levels and more information, look up this title at www.lernerbooks.com.

Main body text set in CC Wild Words.
Typeface provided by Comicraft Design.

Library of Congress Cataloging-in-Publication Data

Robbins, Trina.
        A midterm night's scheme / by Trina Robbins ; illustrated by Tyler Page.
        p.   cm. — (Chicagoland Detective Agency ; #06)
        Summary: Megan's new friend Luna has a mystery for the Chicagoland Detective Agency to solve: who's been following her and stealing the notes for her science fair experiment? Luna's experiment is all about potions.
        ISBN 978-0-7613-8167-9 (lib. bdg. : alk. paper)
        ISBN 978-1-4677-1635-2 (eBook)
        1. Graphic novels. [1. Graphic novels. 2. Mystery and detective stories.
3. Science—Experiments—Fiction. 4. Chicago (Ill.)—Fiction.] I. Page, Tyler, 1976– illustrator. II. Title.
        PZ7.7.R632Mi 2014
        741.5'973—dc23   2012047635

Manufactured in the United States of America
1 – BP – 12/31/13

10

LUNA, CAN YOU THINK OF ANYBODY WHO MIGHT HAVE WANTED TO STEAL YOUR POTIONS?

NOT REALLY, BUT COME TO THINK OF IT, I'VE HAD THIS *FEELING* RECENTLY...

Woof?

...LIKE SOMEBODY IS *FOLLOWING* ME.

AND SOMETIMES IN SCHOOL, I FEEL LIKE SOMEBODY'S *STARING* AT ME.

Ahem, woof, woof?

AHA! THIS IS A JOB FOR MEGAN YAMAMURA, *SUPERSLEUTH* AND TRACER OF *LOST PRINCESSES.*

11

But nobody must know that I, Bradley, the **doggie Einstein,** am the **real** brains behind the Chicagoland Detective Agency.

See, with my extra-sensitive **doggie nose,** I can go to Luna's locker and **sniff** out the culprit.

THEN WE'RE IN **LUCK!** MOST DAYS I CAN'T BRING A DOG TO SCHOOL, BUT WHEN WE HAVE THE **SCIENCE FAIR,** KIDS CAN BRING THEIR FAMILIES AND THEIR DOGS TOO.

MOMMY, THAT DOG WAS TALKING.

DYLAN, DEAR, YOU KNOW DOGS DON'T TALK.

OK, I'LL BE **FOLLOWING** LUNA, BUT I'LL KEEP TO THE **SHADOWS,** SO HER MYSTERY STALKER WON'T SEE ME.

BUT YOU GOTTA STOP **LOOKING BACK** AT ME LIKE THAT, OR YOU'LL GIVE ME AWAY!

SHEESH!

sigh

13

SUSPECT MAKES PURCHASE!
HMM...SLEUTH PREFERRED CUTE NECKLACE...

OOH!

...SUSPECT IS A GIRL!

Bernadette Jablonski (Bernie)
Creative writing club; literary club; winner,
James A. Garfield Poetry contest
My hero: Frida Kahlo. She was so beautiful
and her life was so sad!
"Love is all we need, and then we will have
world peace."

Amanda Jardine "Super Grrrl"
Track, basketball, "The Presidents," James
A. Garfield baseball team
My heroes: Joan of Arc, Gertrude Stein,
Amelia Earhart
"Someday I will be president; then you
won't laugh."

THERE SHE IS, *AMANDA JARDINE.*

Randall Jordan Jr. "Spaz."
After-school "catch up" study group
My heroes: the Joker and the Penguin
"Master criminals are way smarter than
superheroes. Anyway, who needs to spell?"

19

NEVER MIND, I JUST *KNOW* YOU SOLVED THE CASE.

PLUS I MADE YOU SOME *COOKIES*.

THANKS.

SO, RAF, HOW CAN WE *PROVE* SHE DID IT?

AND I BROUGHT SOME *GREEN TEA* TOO, IMPORTED FROM JAPAN, JUST FOR YOU.

ISN'T THAT YOUR FAVORITE?

HUH? YEAH, SURE.

I THINK WE'LL HAVE TO CATCH HER *RED-HANDED.*

WHERE'S THE KITCHEN, RAF?

BACK THERE, LUNA. CUPS ARE ON THE COUNTER.

23

26

29

34

37

41

49

54

Login: chicagoland

Password: •••••••n|

Click here to interFACE

MYBLOGFACE

CHICAGOLAND DETECTIVE AGENCY

InforFACEtion

Location: Behind the counter of Hernandez & Sons Pet Supply store

Hours: 9–5 during summer vacation. During the rest of the year, after-school hours, except on weekends.

Proprietor: Raf Hernandez (that's me) because it's my mom's store

Our motto:

Sad? Scared? Need help fast?
Chicagoland Detectives:
We can do the job!

The Chicagoland Detective Agency is here for you. We solve low crimes and misdemeanors, and we battle injustice. Don't be afraid to come in with your pets. We love animals.

Friendly FACErs

38 Friends

 Bradley

 Megan Yamamura

William Johnson

Amanda Jardine

 Luna Zimmerman

Chicagoland BLOG ENTRY #6

FIND IT AT THE LIBRARY!

By Raf Hernandez

For my last birthday, my mom gave me a gift card for that Internet auction site, HighEstate.net, but Bradley used up all the credit buying rare old reference books that we used to help solve our cases. So when I needed to get a book on spells and potions, instead of buying the book, I looked in our public library.

The library is amazing! They have books on every subject, more than anyone could ever read in their whole lifetime, and you can borrow them for free. But remember that you have to return the books in good condition and on time. Those overdue fees sure add up! So don't bend down the pages or underline words or anything! When Megan was mixing up that anti-potion witch's brew, I was afraid she'd splash it all over the book, but Bradley was careful not to get the book too close to the stove.

I'm a lucky kid. When I was five years old, my mom discovered that I was writing math problems on her computer, so she bought me one of my own. But not all kids are so lucky, and not all moms and dads can afford to buy a computer for their kids, so here's more good news about libraries: they have computers for kids (grown-ups too!) to use free.

So next time you need to do research or you just want something fun to read, find it at the library!

Megan Yamamura
Age: 13½

Education: Stepford
Preparatory Academy

Profession: Detective

Guest Blogger: Megan Yamamura ☒

I guess by now you know that witches are not crooked-nosed, warty, green women in pointy hats. And they're not devil worshippers either, but that's what people believed long ago. In 1692, four preteen girls caused a mass hysteria in Salem, Massachusetts, when they accused people of being witches and the villagers believed them. (I know, the villagers were as crazy as those girls!) By the time the craziness was over, nearly two hundred people, mostly women, had been accused of worshipping the devil, and twenty of them had been hanged. As for those girls who started it all, some people will do anything to get attention!

Anyway, having been a preteen girl myself just a year ago, I think those four girls in Salem were a disgrace to the name of preteen girls everywhere, so I have composed an angry haiku:

BAD GIRLS, SHAME ON YOU!
DISGRACING ALL PRETEEN GIRLS,
BAD GIRLS, YOU'RE GROUNDED!

Today most witches prefer to be called Wiccans, and if they worship anything, it's Earth and nature and animals, so they tend to be very nice people, like Luna. If you want to find out more about Wicca and Wiccans, you know where to go: the library!

Amanda Jardine
Age: 13
Education: James A. Garfield Middle School

Guest Blogger: Amanda Jardine ⊠

The Chicagoland Detective Agency totally rules! If not for you guys, I would never have had the courage to tell Luna how I felt about her or to give her the Magic Eight Ball I bought for her. (Of course, I then found out that real witches don't use stuff like Magic Eight Balls but whatever.)

Anyway, this whole experience has taught me something: If you really like somebody, you should tell them, instead of following them around like a lovesick puppy, like I did. Plus, following people around can get you in trouble. Look what happened to me: I almost got accused of a crime I didn't commit!

Luna Zimmerman
Age: 13
Education: James A. Garfield Middle School

Guest Blogger: Luna Zimmerman ⊠

The Chicagoland Detective Agency is awesome, and I want to thank them for solving the case of the missing potions, plus getting Amanda Jardine and me together.

But I'd also like to explain something: That Magic Eight Ball that Amanda gave me is just a fun toy, not real magic. If you've never seen one, it's a big black ball with a small transparent window on the bottom. The way it works is you hold it with the window away from you and ask it a question. Then you turn it toward you and see the answer float into the window. Some people shake it, but that just causes bubbles.

Even though we real witches never use toys like the Magic Eight Ball to read fortunes, it was very sweet of Amanda to give me one.

Advertisement